The Jolt Felt Around the World

Susanna Shetley

Illustrated by Krystal Smith

The Jolt Felt Around the World

Published by Wisdom House Books, Inc.
Chapel Hill, North Carolina 27514 USA · 919.883.4669
www.wisdomhousebooks.com

Wisdom House Books is committed to excellence in the publishing industry.

Cover and Interior Illustrations by Krystal Smith
Interior and Cover design by Lindi Kistler

Published in the United States of America

Hardback ISBN: 978-1-7336573-0-3
LCCN: 2019917391

1. JUV039220 | JUVENILE FICTION / Social Themes / Values & Virtues
2. JUV039250 | JUVENILE FICTION / Social Themes / Emigration & Immigration
3. JUV063000 | JUVENILE FICTION / Recycling & Green Living

First Edition

14 13 12 11 10 / 10 9 8 7 6 5 4 3 2 1

This is a story of misunderstanding, compassion, and hope.

Dedicated to my late mother, Brenda Shetley, a career librarian and lifelong lover of books, the one who read to me as a child and showed me how to chase big dreams. Mom, this book is for you.

Mother Earth was sick and dirty.
Her vibrant blues and greens were dull
and growing duller each day.

One could look high and low, left and right,
but there was no more room for trash.

The gunk weighed down Earth so
heavily, she began to fall from the sky.
It happened quietly one day.
Earthlings felt a jolt.
It was only one, but something about
it felt strange.

Days later, another was felt—more intense this time.
Meteorologists reported them as earthquakes,
but they didn't feel like earthquakes.
It wasn't a shaking feeling;
it was a dropping feeling.
And it was felt around the entire world.

Space satellites researched the situation.
NASA was struck with fear at what they saw.
Earth was no longer in the right spot!
Not even the strong pull of gravity could hold
up so much waste.

Leaders from around the
globe met to devise a plan.
They put their heads together
but couldn't agree on a clear way
to keep Earth from falling.
They didn't have enough time or
knowledge to remove the trash.

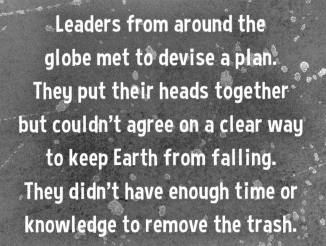

There was only one solution:
Earthlings would have to flee
to other planets.

Venus and Mars were closest to Earth,
so Earth's leaders sent pleading messages
to these two planets, asking if Earthlings
could relocate.

Venus replied first, and said,
"I'm sorry, but no, you cannot move here. Fifteen
years ago, we were in trouble and in need
of fresh water, but you would not send your
brilliant minds to help us."

Mars then responded,
"For decades, you've made fun of us by saying
we're inferior to you. You've reported we aren't
capable of sustaining life.
Why would we welcome you with open arms?"

The leaders were in shock. Earth had always been the wealthiest, healthiest, most progressive planet in the galaxy. Shouldn't the rest of the solar system be honored to help? The Earthling leaders shook off the rejection and sent two new messages. This time, they contacted Saturn and Jupiter.

With these two planets being so large,
perhaps they wouldn't mind a few billion
Earthlings taking up a little room.

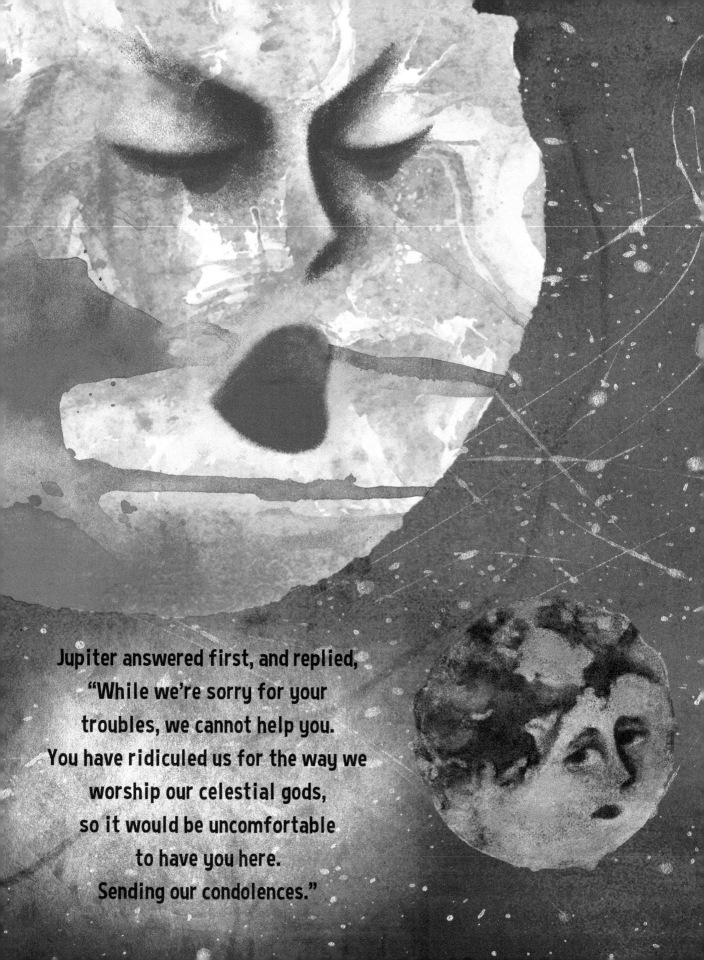

Jupiter answered first, and replied,
"While we're sorry for your
troubles, we cannot help you.
You have ridiculed us for the way we
worship our celestial gods,
so it would be uncomfortable
to have you here.
Sending our condolences."

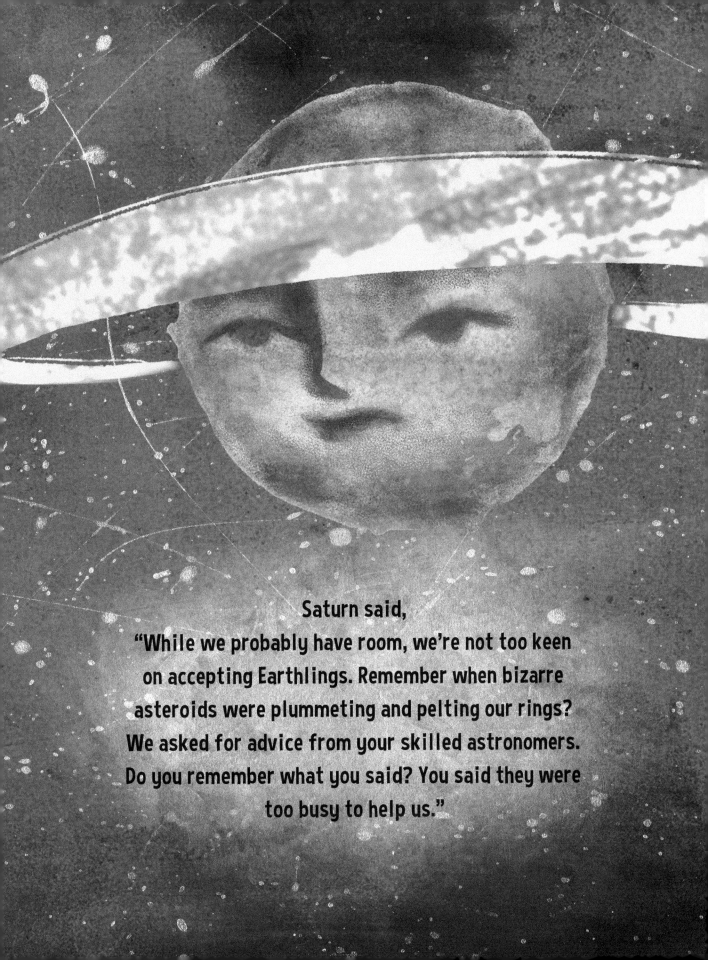

Saturn said,
"While we probably have room, we're not too keen
on accepting Earthlings. Remember when bizarre
asteroids were plummeting and pelting our rings?
We asked for advice from your skilled astronomers.
Do you remember what you said? You said they were
too busy to help us."

Earth's leaders became frantic.
The Earthlings were looking
to them for a solution!

Every day, the dropping feeling became more and more extreme.

Next, the leaders contacted Mercury.
Mercury had fewer inhabitants than any other planet,
so maybe they could help.

Mercury quickly replied with a message:
"A while back, we wanted you to move some of
your Earthlings to our planet.
We sought more diversity, so we asked the
overpopulated planets to offer a handful of
beings to Mercury.
Every planet complied but you.
Now, we're a thriving melting pot of a planet,
so we're in no need of new inhabitants."

Hesitantly, the leaders contacted Neptune and Uranus. Earth had a history of conflict with them, but they were their last options.

As expected, Neptune and Uranus were still wounded from Earth's past actions, and said, "We know what it feels like to need refuge. We can't, in good conscience, welcome you here when you rejected us in our greatest time of crisis."

Earth's leaders were extraordinarily concerned.
In their heart of hearts, they began
to feel guilty for not helping the other planets.

Then, they got a surprise message from Pluto.
The message read:

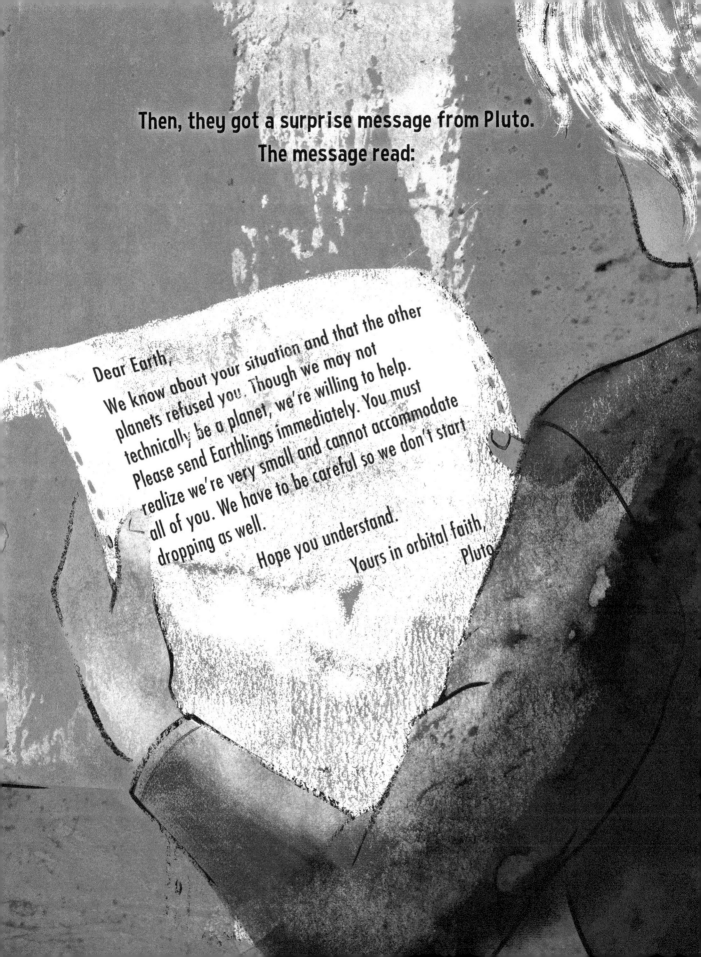

Dear Earth,

We know about your situation and that the other planets refused you. Though we may not technically be a planet, we're willing to help. Please send Earthlings immediately. You must realize we're very small and cannot accommodate all of you. We have to be careful so we don't start dropping as well.

Hope you understand.

Yours in orbital faith,
Pluto

This message gave the leaders some reassurance.

Pluto didn't specify who should come. Since the leaders knew it would be chaos trying to decide who should go and who should stay, they kept Pluto's offering a secret and sent only themselves.

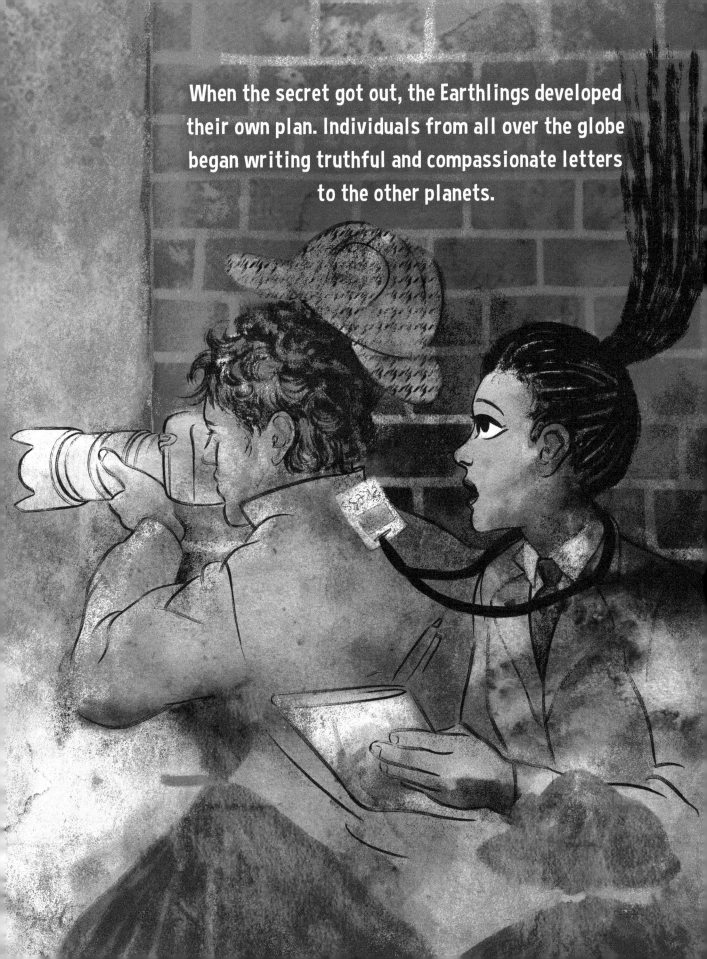

When the secret got out, the Earthlings developed their own plan. Individuals from all over the globe began writing truthful and compassionate letters to the other planets.

The letters said things like:

"Venus, my name is Celia. Common Earthlings never knew you needed hydrologists. I study water cycles and would've happily visited to help you find fresh water. For what it's worth, I'd still love to do that!"

"Hi there, Mars! I'm Ben. On behalf of everyone, I apologize if it seemed like we were making fun of you. There's actually an entire population of people who adore you. We're called sci-fi junkies. I would give anything to visit you, meet your beings, and explore the planet."

"Jupiter, my name is Mishka. I studied religion in college and am intrigued by your phrase 'celestial gods.' On behalf of all good Earthlings, I'm sorry if you thought we disapproved of how you worship.

Even though our leaders don't show it, our world embraces more religions than I can describe in this letter."

"Greetings, Saturn! My name is Margaret, and I've worked with NASA for twenty-five years. I was never told you needed advice about your rings.

While I love my job, I feel like something is missing. I've never taken on a key project and would love to visit Saturn with my best team!"

"Dear Uranus, my name is Rebekkah. Though we knew about Neptune needing refuge, no one even told us about your troubles. Whether you allow any of us to come or not, we send peaceful and loving wishes."

When the other planets received these messages and others like them, their hearts softened. They now understood that the small group of leaders did not reflect the humanity of Earth. Together, they discussed the letters and Earth's dire situation. They voted to let the Earthlings relocate until Earth was restored.

Meanwhile, Earth's leaders
heard what Earthlings had done
and were impressed.

They realized they didn't
always know best and should
listen to common Earthlings
more often.

Over the following weeks,
Earthlings moved to various planets.

And then, something beautiful happened.
Within the coming years, all of the planets came
together to save Mother Earth.

Teams of the galaxy's best researchers, scientists,
and environmentalists worked around the clock to restore
Earth's health so she could thrive as she once did.

And Earthlings could, again, call her home.

About the Author

Susanna Shetley has been writing since childhood, where a napkin or scrap of paper was all that was needed to create a story. She has always loved working with kids, and taught middle school language arts until becoming a dedicated full-time writer, parenting blogger, and speaker. With her children as her greatest inspiration, she decided to combine her passions for writing, education, and helping others to make the world a better place one book at a time.

Susanna and her two young sons live in the Blue Ridge Mountains with their cat, Oliver.

About the Illustrator

Krystal Smith is a designer, artist, and recipient of a BFA in Illustration from the Maryland Institute College of Art (MICA) in Baltimore, Maryland. She was a winner in the 2016 Society of Illustrators Student Competition in New York, NY and has had her work shown across the east coast in Florida, Maryland, New York, and North Carolina.

CPSIA information can be obtained
at www.ICGtesting.com
Printed in the USA
BVHW020739231119
564027BV00007B/6/P